In the memory of our LOVE

TAHSEEN SHAH

BLUEROSE PUBLISHERS
India | U.K.

Copyright © Tahseen Shah 2024

All rights reserved by author. No part of this publication may be reproduced, stored in a retrieval system or transmitted in any form or by any means, electronic, mechanical, photocopying, recording or otherwise, without the prior permission of the author. Although every precaution has been taken to verify the accuracy of the information contained herein, the publisher assume no responsibility for any errors or omissions. No liability is assumed for damages that may result from the use of information contained within.

BlueRose Publishers takes no responsibility for any damages, losses, or liabilities that may arise from the use or misuse of the information, products, or services provided in this publication.

For permissions requests or inquiries regarding this publication, please contact:

BLUEROSE PUBLISHERS
www.BlueRoseONE.com
info@bluerosepublishers.com
+91 8882 898 898
+4407342408967

ISBN: 978-93-5989-333-4

Cover design: Tahira
Typesetting: Tanya Raj Upadhyay

First Edition: February 2024

Intro

I'm Shahzaib, a teenager writing a book about my life. Before I met the love of my life, everything was going well in my life. However, the moment I learned about her, everything changed. She was the most ideal girl, supporting me when I needed it and helping me with my studies. You will accompany me in heaven, Shahzaib, and even if you don't meet the academic goals you set for yourself, I will still be with you. She will undoubtedly be the princess of heaven, but I don't deserve it. I could write a ton of books for you. The most exquisite creation ever made in such a delicate way gripped me so tightly both physically and emotionally, but the circumstances were harsh and prevented us from being together. If you ever read it, you should know that my feelings for you were sincere.

Other than I have got friends but not too close to them And my parents are the most strict and unsupportive parents I have ever seen.

Table of Contents

First reflection 1
Angel in disguise... 2
Company 3
Age of misery.. 4
Trauma 5
Closure.. 6
My twin angels 7
Accepted 8
Complexity 9
With you..10
Temporary things 11
Promise..12
Nothing 13
Truth 14
You...15
Likewise...16
Late night 17
Past..18
Wishes 19
Time 20
Quote...21
Quote...22
Quote...23
Aftermath 24
The last message..25
May be 26
Note...27
Advice..28

First reflection

When I saw you for the first time
It was like I saw the most beautiful thing of my life
May be not more than a paradise but still the best thing of my life
Why did God create you with so much beauty
Probably to refresh my aching heart
You indeed were a medication to relieve my hearts tension

Is my mind playing tricks on me or is it the beauty of your eyes that is drowning me inside
Death? probably the best demise a person could get
In your face I find solace
May you be protected from worlds filthiness
Because you are the thing to be cherished by the best

Angel in disguise

You never know how beautiful you are, take my eyes and see the world. You will see a whole new universe. Maybe you are the tiny particle of it but the most beautiful in it. You are the charm that my luck needed because you completed my life in the slightest of time ,my little princess

Company

They lie to me
They all do
Snakes they are called
Trying to bite me with twisted fangs
Do they know resistant I am to their treacherous schemes

Age of misery

Parents' blessings of God?
Punishment they are for killing our dreams
Yet they say we love our queens
Is love really so painful?
For this should I be grateful?
Is their love so costly?
That you have to let your dreams flee

For those who understand their children
Indeed, you have a very good vision
Love your children by loving their dreams
Otherwise, you will never hear the screams

Trauma

Everyone may not understand
Neither will everyone take your stand
It is an ailment of great mischief
Some say yes some say no
But in the end, you are the one fighting alone
It is like carrying a mountain on your head
Beneath it you are a walking dead

Neither you can live nor you can die
Tell the one who is above the sky
Why are you making me cry?
My apologies for questioning God
But is this what humans have been made for?

Closure

No one is there to trust my issues
Secluded I am from the company of world
Talkative I was when a child
No one talks to me as going by
It's been rough like a prisoner in jail
Who is the one giving me bail?

Alone I stand in the sunless world
Is there someone who will lend me ear
Or I have to live always in fear

Fear of not being understood
May be a rebellious child
But I will rise and shine
And make you understand the difficulty of mine

My twin angels

They came to my life as a source of light
OH! Shahzaib the only thing that you like
Are the twin angels of your life
Their helping hand came to you in a ditch of night
You can never pay for the light
Showering you with sight
So that you can light

Accepted

It was the day when the wind was very gentle
flashing in my mind was your imagination
Suddenly came to me a piece of information
You were ready to be mine which was against God's consideration

You fought along me the barrier of age Now came angels pursuing God's message
Formidable was our attack to put them away
Now came to me an enigma thought: is it ok to be untrue to the originator?

Complexity

I was delirious the whole time
Pondering would you be mine
Searching for a sign
Came to me a twinkling thought
Why would you choose me in a cluster of lamps
Shining so bright they are with their light
There is me with withered sight

With you

Moment of magic you are
Making me feel special at any cost
You make me feel safe
You make my home comfortable
I wish this is not a dream
But the dream is beautiful
With you I feel might
With you I feel alive

I wish this journey never ends
May It end with our sunshine
Taking care of us in our old age
Making us proud

I wish you by my side
Taking care of me when I stumble
Giving me the courage to fight
Giving me love when I am fragile

In the nature we will fly
I will make every moment count
Feeling so special to be with you
I will always, will you?

Temporary things

Why should I care for friends when I have got you
They are not true as you
Maybe my shortcomings! why should I care when I have got you
They are near but still not there
While in your absence I find you here
They don't count me as a friend
Yet you consider me as your eternal end

Promise

My promise wasn't enough
Cherishing you was very tough
OH! God why can't I hate her?
God to me in human form
Was my worship not enough but yes it was very tough

Like a seedling I wanted to grow under your shade
Wanted you to be an arborist shaping me in the best possible way
You were a woodcutter cutting me
Leaving me to bleed and plea

Nothing

Solitude brings me pleasure
Some go on enjoying with too much noise
While you shahzaib are writing
Writing your own dreams
Which will never be fulfilled
In my own space I have made solitude my friend
A place where my soul can mend

Truth

I shall wait for you above the sky
Do come alone when you die
We will be together in paradise
Roaming around with no one to care
Holding hands, we will dance
Joyful will be the moment you arrive
Know that in paradise our love will thrive

You

Immortal you will be always
In my poems of misery
When you look into them do think of me

Your name will always be taken with shahzaib
Though not in destiny

Likewise

Forever is a joke in my generation
Hookup is our only satisfaction
Poetry gives me the power to unleash my pain
And gives me the solace once again

People think you are mad oh shahzaib
When will they understand you are in pain

Never settle in the rhythm of love
Cause it is fake at every occasion

Late night

The unfulfilled wish of mine you are
The most distinguishing thing you are
Only God knows who will get you
But he will be grateful to have you

God did create lucky ones
He will be lucky too

For you I would have destroyed the world
But you never gave me a chance to

The one who will meet your gaze will dive deep in the ocean of emotions

Maybe he will find me
Or the person who lost you?

In this world of unfulfilled love story
I turned ours into a masterpiece of misery

Past

Knowing the present
May be not wanting to meet you
Yet I had to
You were a masterpiece of God
How could I not

Life was simple before everything
Not knowing shahzaib will turn into a poet of misery

You were a mystery to be solved
A story to be lived
Yet the life was simple
Simple as the flow of river

Life was uncomplicated
Until shahzaib became a poet of sorrow

Life once simple
As serene as flowing river

Wishes

To live in your dreams is what I want
Ringing the bell is what I stopped
My wishes were too heavy for the eternal one
Loving you alone will be my destiny
For sure I could move on
But living in your memories is paradise for me
Why should I leave my paradise?
And wait for someone's smile that is not guaranteed
And leave your sight which still beautifies me

Time

How lucky I am to live in the same life time as you
Unlucky I am not to have spent it with you
Yes, I am in love the world will know
But I will be watching them from above
They didn't care for me when I was alive
Maybe they will with my demise

Quote

I will be remembered forever as your lover
And someone will have the honour to be called your better half. It doesn't defame me but was it my place?

Quote

Sometimes we think our love story will be remembered for ever only to discover it has become an immortal piece of reference

Quote

Sometimes we believe we are the reason for each other's living only to find out they were looking for someone else's well being

Aftermath

You were the reason
That I believed in love
You were the reason
That showed me how
You were like a drug
A necessity to me
Killing me from inside
But still keeping me alive

You were the reason
I enjoyed life
Still cannot believe
That you are out of sight
You were the reason
That gave me might
You deserved to be
At my greatest heights

The last message

Whoa! My heart's regret
You arrived like breeze in the wintry air
God's design never changed even as the season did
You were a king's palace and an orphan's refuge
The finest possible thing I could have
I'll battle the might of fate in different universe and use all my strength to hug you close

May be

In the realm of dark
Lies a beautiful secret
Secret that will unfold thousands of mysteries
Mysteries that are yet to be unveiled
May be in short term we will meet again
And write a new story that may want us to meet again
A side of me that is captivating
It is dark
But I hope you find it kind

Note

From Amila: We'll cross paths once more. I'll look over your records, and perhaps in the future we can be together. But for now, that's not possible. If you look for me, you'll find me above the mountains, where secrets will be revealed and a riddle will be solved.

Advice

Seen so much rejection
Yet heart is not at tension
Had to go through a lot
But I just want
You have the might to choose the right
Yet you live in delusion your whole life

Be at patience
That is the life's rule
No, you will not fail
If you choose the right direction

www.ingramcontent.com/pod-product-compliance
Lightning Source LLC
LaVergne TN
LVHW061605070526
838199LV00077B/7184